Goat and Donkey
in Strawberry Sunglasses

For John Brown and Norman Taylor, with big thanks – S.P.

For Freeman and Beryl Julian, and Eric and 'Midge' Bonsor, the perfect grandparents – R.J.

OXFORD
UNIVERSITY PRESS
Great Clarendon Street, Oxford OX2 6DP

Oxford University Press is a department of the University of Oxford.
It furthers the University's objective of excellence in research, scholarship,
and education by publishing worldwide in

Oxford New York
Auckland Cape Town Dar es Salaam Hong Kong Karachi
Kuala Lumpur Madrid Melbourne Mexico City Nairobi
New Delhi Shanghai Taipei Toronto

With offices in
Argentina Austria Brazil Chile Czech Republic France Greece
Guatemala Hungary Italy Japan Poland Portugal Singapore
South Korea Switzerland Thailand Turkey Ukraine Vietnam

Oxford is a registered trade mark of Oxford University Press
in the UK and in certain other countries

Text copyright © Simon Puttock 2007
Illustrations copyright © Russell Julian 2007

The moral rights of the author and artist have been asserted

Database right Oxford University Press (maker)

First published 2007

British Library Cataloguing in Publication Data available

ISBN 978-0-19-279195-5 (Hardback)
ISBN 978-0-19-272599-8 (Paperback)

10 9 8 7 6 5 4 3 2 1

Printed in Singapore

Simon Puttock and Russell Julian

Goat and Donkey
in Strawberry Sunglasses

OXFORD
UNIVERSITY PRESS

'Goodness,' said Donkey one morning, 'there is nothing to eat! The cupboard is BARE. I really must go shopping today, but I am so busy!'

'Oh, Donkey,' said Goat. 'I will go shopping for you. I am GOOD at shopping.' Now, Donkey knew that Goat was often muddly and forgetful. But they were best friends, and Donkey also knew that best friends must be thoughtful and kind to each other.

'Are you SURE?' he asked, 'because you might get in a muddle.' 'Today,' said Goat, 'I will not be muddly AT ALL!'

'Then I will make a list,' said Donkey,
'and you must buy just what is on it.'
'Goody,' said Goat.

Donkey wrote the list. He wrote:
ten rosy apples
eight juicy carrots
four crunchy cabbages
any flavour ice cream.
'You can choose the ice cream,' said Donkey.
'I like strawberry best!' said Goat.
'Splendid,' said Donkey. 'So do I.'

Goat fetched the shopping basket, and trotted off to town.
When he got to the market, there was so
much to look at! All the stalls had such
wonderful, colourful things to buy,
it made Goat feel quite giddy.

A jazzy clothes stall caught Goat's eye.
He stopped to look, and saw a beautiful sun hat.
That would be just the thing for Donkey! he thought,
and he looked at the shopping list. But Donkey's writing
was very grown up, and difficult to read. Goat looked
at it so long, he got muddled.

One beautiful sun hat, he decided, was just
what Donkey had put on the list. So he bought it.

Goat trotted along the market lanes. A swimmy, seaside
sort of stall caught his eye. Goat stopped to look,
and saw an orange blow-up octopus.
That would be just the thing to have at the beach,
thought Goat, and he looked at the shopping list.

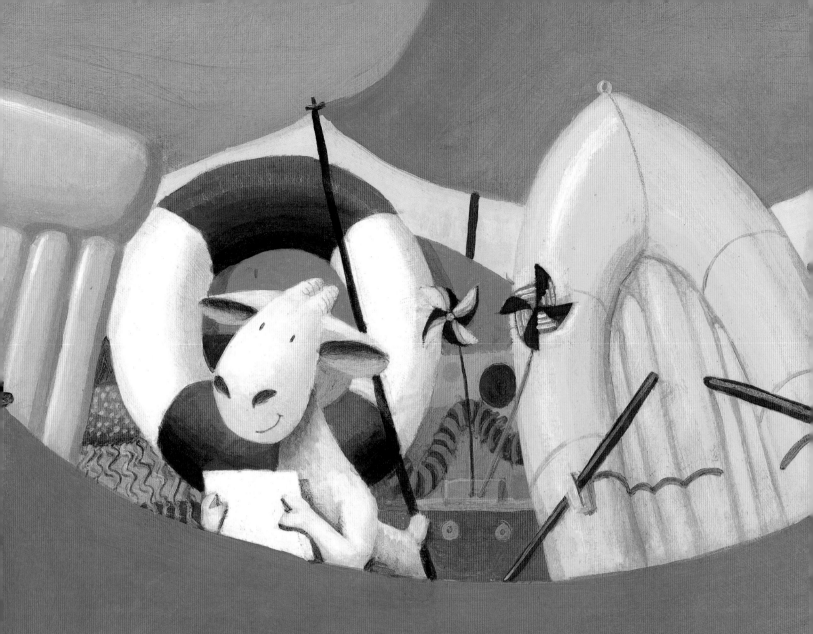

'Oh dear,' said Goat, 'what DOES it say?'
And though he tried not to, he got muddled again.

One orange blow-up octopus, he decided, was just
what Donkey had put on the list. So he bought it.

Goat trotted along the market lanes. A musical sort of stall caught his eye. Goat stopped to look, and saw a shiny, golden trumpet. I bet Donkey would LOVE to toot on that! thought Goat, and he looked at Donkey's shopping list. Really, thought Goat, Donkey should write more NEATLY! I can't read this AT ALL! And, of course, he got muddled AGAIN!

One shiny, golden trumpet, he decided, was just
what Donkey had put on the list. So he bought it.

Now, thought Goat, I have just one more thing to buy.
And it has something to do with . . . strawberries!
Goat trotted along the market lanes. An odds-and-ends sort
of stall caught his eye. Goat stopped to look, and he saw
a pair of green sunglasses with real plastic strawberries on them.

They were VERY smart! Goat longed to try them on.

Of course! thought Goat. Strawberries!
How clever of Donkey. That must be
EXACTLY what he put on the list.
And he bought the
strawberry sunglasses
right away.

Then Goat trotted happily home.

When Donkey saw all the things that Goat had bought,
he WAS surprised. 'Oh, Goat!' he said. 'You HAVE
got muddled! Where are the apples and carrots
and cabbages and ice cream for supper?'

Goat's face fell.
'Oh,' he said, feeling rather foolish.
'I had a little trouble with the list.'

'I guessed as much,' said Donkey.
Then he put on his sun hat and tooted his trumpet,
to show Goat how pleased he was to have them.

'But,' said Donkey, 'we STILL don't have anything for supper. We will go shopping TOGETHER and, this time, I will help you.'
'Goody,' said Goat, 'yes, let's!'

And that is (almost) exactly what they did.